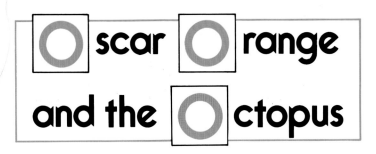

Oscar Orange and the Octopus

Written by Stephanie Laslett
Illustrated by Maggie Downer

Collins

An imprint of HarperCollins*Publishers*

It was a lovely day down at the
Letterland Docks. The sun shone,
the blue sea sparkled and the
seagulls squawked happily. But Oscar
Orange was too busy to notice.
A cargo of socks had just arrived.

"Look, Mr O," cried Oscar. "Lots and
lots of socks!"
But Mr O spotted a problem.
"These socks need sorting out. Can you
pack them in pairs in this oblong box?"
"Oh, no," groaned Oscar. "What a job!"

Soon there were socks all over the dock.
"I'll help you, Oscar," called a voice.
It was a small brown otter with quick
neat paws.
"Yes please!" said Oscar.

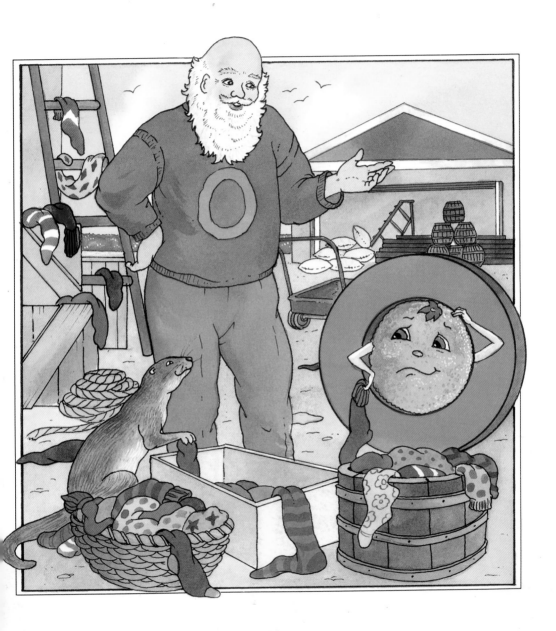

"One sock, two socks," counted Oscar. He laid the matching pairs on the dock beside the box.

The otter packed them away in the box. Suddenly he stopped. "Here's an odd sock. Where is the other one?"

Oscar could not understand it. He had sorted all the socks into pairs and now one sock had gone. What *was* going on? "Never mind," said Oscar. "We must carry on."

The otter and Oscar got on with their job, but soon the otter shouted out again. "Stop, stop. Here is another odd sock." Oscar was puzzled. "This odd sock mystery is very … odd!" he said.

Just then a strange noise came from behind a large wooden box.

Oscar peeped behind the box and saw a very odd looking object. It had a large round head, two shiny black eyes and eight long arms.

"Hello," said the creature. "I am an octopus." Then Oscar spotted his missing socks on the ends of the octopus arms.

"These are my tentacles," said the octopus happily. "I wanted a sock for each one. Don't they look jolly?"

"No, they do not," said Oscar crossly. "I need those socks to finish my job." The octopus looked very sorry. "Time to be off," he said.

Soon Oscar had finished his job. "Well done, Oscar," said Mr O. "You did so well that I think you could look after my dock on your own." "On my own?" gasped Oscar.

"My friend Captain Cockle is off to the Boat Show," explained Mr O. "He has invited me to go, too. I will be back tomorrow afternoon. Can I leave you in charge?"

"No problem," replied Oscar. "Now off you go, Mr O, or you'll miss the boat."

Mr O waved as the boat steamed from the harbour. "Remember, Oscar," he called. "You're the boss." "Don't worry, Mr O," replied Oscar. "I'll keep your dock looking tip-top."

That night Oscar slept like a log.
Bright and early next morning
he was down at the dock.

"What jobs have I got today?" he
wondered as he looked at Mr O's
Office book. "A boat full of oranges
to offload at one o'clock. That's good.
Plenty of time to mop the dock."

Soon Oscar was busy with lots of hot
soapy water and a big floppy mop.
From nine o'clock to twelve o'clock
he did not stop.

"Gosh, I'm hot!" cried Oscar, as
he mopped his brow with a spotty
handkerchief. "Time to stop."
He flopped into a chair and soon
nodded off.

One hour later Oscar was woken by a loud "Toot, toot!" "It's the one o'clock orange boat," he cried as he ran down to the dock.

"Ready to offload the cargo, boss," called the Captain. "Where's the crane operator?"

"That's me!" replied Oscar, excitedly. He hopped behind the crane controls and had soon hooked up the large net full of juicy oranges.

"Going up!" shouted Oscar, as the crane lifted the oranges off the deck. "Going down!" he yelled as he lowered the net on to the dock.

S uddenly something went wrong. Oscar spotted a hole at the top of the net.
"The rope knot is coming undone!" he cried. With a loud rip, the net tore open and hundreds of oranges dropped all over the dock.

What a shock! Oranges everywhere! "Stop, stop!" howled Oscar. "Oranges overboard!" The oranges overflowed the dock and dropped into the sea — plop, plop, plop.

"Golly, what a problem," shouted Oscar, as he hopped up and down among the oranges. "Mr O will be cross!"

O scar rushed around the dock picking up oranges and piling them into boxes.
"I'll never get them all," he cried. Suddenly he sat down and sobbed and sobbed and sobbed.

Oscar was so busy crying that he didn't see a strange shape rising up out of the sea behind him. Water trickled off its shiny round head and its two large black eyes twinkled. Two long arms picked up two oranges from the sea and gently put them on the dock beside Oscar.

Oscar slowly turned round. There was the octopus with oranges bobbing all around him.

"I am sorry I borrowed your socks," said the octopus. "But now I know how I can help. It's obvious. You need an octopus on the job!"

"Of course!" cried Oscar, happily. "I have only got two arms and I'm much too slow. You have got eight arms — let's see *you* have a go!"

The octopus worked non-stop. His long arms scooped all the oranges from the sea and dropped them beside Oscar. Then he climbed on to the dock to help. His eight strong arms filled box after box with oranges.

"Fantastic!" shouted Oscar. "Don't stop! Don't stop!"

In no time at all every orange was packed in a box.
"Thank goodness," said Oscar.

Just then they heard a loud "toot, toot".

"Here comes Mr O!"

"You have done a good job, Oscar," said Mr O as he stepped ashore. "My dock looks spotless and the orange boxes are all in order."

"Well, we had a spot of bother," admitted Oscar. "But I had the best dockworker in the world to help me. Meet my friend, the octopus."

"Hello, hello!" laughed Mr O, shaking two octopus tentacles at once. "Oscar is a great help to me here at the Docks, but I could do with someone like you to lend an extra hand — or eight! Could I offer you a job?"

The octopus looked very pleased. He nodded so hard that Oscar thought his head would drop off!

"Welcome to the Docks," said Mr O. "And now it's time for a nice cool drink. Orange juice, anyone?"

"No, thank you, Mr O!" groaned Oscar.

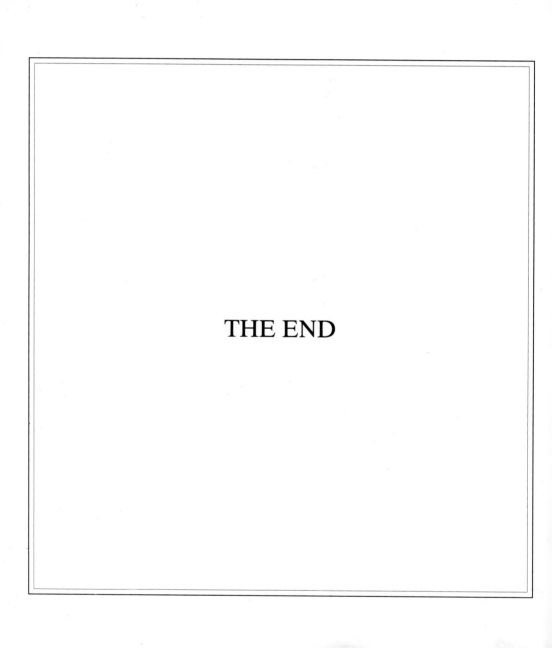

THE END